TO BE YOU: THE BEGINNING

WE MARCH BY CLONES

MASONIA WILLIAMS

authorHOUSE

AuthorHouse™
1663 Liberty Drive
Bloomington, IN 47403
www.authorhouse.com
Phone: 833-262-8899

Published by AuthorHouse 05/26/2021

ISBN: 978-1-6655-2468-1 (sc)
ISBN: 978-1-6655-2469-8 (hc)
ISBN: 978-1-6655-2467-4 (e)

Library of Congress Control Number: 2021908876

CHAPTER 1

WHO ARE YOU?

INTRODUCTION

A world filled with clones but controlled by humans with an unexpected twist. The Vegan Family is in for one hell of a ride once their own clones go against them. A betrayal that is known for war.

1

Soldiers of clones marched outside the Vegan's clones Technology Hospital, on private land, where no one knew existed.

A clone airplane made out of technology by a remote control, controlled by humans, or were they human? Their heads turned as dolls. The airplane slowly ascended upward. A Lincoln Town Car pulled up, headlights on. A woman in heels steps out of the car, bare legs touching each other while standing by the car. The car door slams shut while the woman walks forward inside the hospital. Nobody saw her face or what she looked like.

Face yourself in the mirror and begin to see what you are and what you believe in.

The wind blows through the midnight rain, cars passing by, traffic disturbing. The mirror fades and just stands off. Chelsa places her lipstick on the corner of the sink. She stands there and just becomes more different and more distant from what she really was and is. An instant killer that just kills. A man back behind of Chelsa closest to her than ever. He kisses her, she turns around but nothing there. Music plays in the background. She looks at her phone, her fake nails touching the wooden desk of her father. She looks out the window and just sighs as she turns around hearing the violin to the song that was playing.

Victoria texts her messages.
Where are you? Your money is here
Why is Kristen in the hospital?
What did you do?
Who are you?

No reply from Chelsa. Chelsa looks at the messages and began to text but didn't. She places the phone down and began to look at New York as she looks out the window. She began to twist her hips to the song that was playing. The door knocks, but she didn't respond. Chelsa began to jump out the window and land down to her feet as she landed to the next building with her backpack, phone in pocket, ipod still in her hand, music still playing. She looks at the other window she jumped out of by another building 20 inches into the air. She looks at her father as she holds the see through rifle that she was about to shoot out of. He finally looks her way, she shoots fire one in the head, one on the side. Chelsa smirks and just began to walk as the building blows up while she walks and just jumps to the next building. She stands around waiting for the package that just arrived brought in by the girl Chelsa met at the bar 5 nights ago. She puts her blonde hair in a business like ponytail. She began to count when the woman was going to show her the money but she showed up at the right time. I knew you were here. Victoria. Chelsa. Nice meeting you says Chelsa and Victoria as they said together at the same time. The money is in here. Chelsa gave Victoria her cut and walked away. When Victoria looked away a gun cocked behind her.

The technology went off as soon as the technology professor lost control of the robot. The real humans were captured by clones while the clone humans were out and about. Different humans were detected by technology. Nobody knew what was real and what wasn't. It took human blood and batteries to make another human clone. Chelsa hugs Victoria and began to run and jump to the next building and lands 50 to 90 feet down from the city building onto the car downtown. People murmuring things that they couldn't believe. The man that saw was shocked and was excited to meet her but as soon as he saw her, most of her skin was peeling off as a robot, live skin pulsing out as a heartbeat would when it was out of breath.

Hello, my name is Chelsa. How are you? She asked nicely. I'm good, he answered excitedly. I'm good. Chelsa shook his hand. What are you doing? Jerry asks with a smile. You know something, you're kind of cute. Oh yeah? Chelsa questioned. He says curiously but happy. Here is my number. He didn't know her but felt moved by her. He loved her hugs. She was definitely a killer but couldn't kill him. The answer was why?

Kora sits down in her room, sitting right by the window. A butcher knife besides her, shining through the room. Kora smiles as she waited for her cousin to come in. Blena comes into the room, unaware of who was in the room. Kora purposely knocks down the wine glass that was beside her on the table. Blena jumps up and then touches her heart as it heated faster then it's normal rate.

"Did I scare you?." asked Kora

"Bitch, Please." Blena said closing the door. Glancing at Kora, Kora glancing back at her and then rolled her eyes back to her knife.

"Do you even know how to use that thing?" asked Blena sarcastically.

"Do you?." Kora asked calmly, folding her legs. Blena turned on the tv, turning the channels aggressively trying to find the ABC news. As soon as it was turned on the channel, the news reporters were stating that two officers were shot by human clones. Kora leans forward to the television while Blena stood still watching, and at the Grand Hotel two clone humans were killed on the 18th floor. Kora sighs as she wipes down the table.

The Technology hospital was losing control of their robots and needed more authorities to stop them but of course the authorities were clones as well, with batteries. So, anything that happened it was out of anybody's control.

2

FIND ME IF YOU CAN

Chelsa lies in the bed with a smile as she arrives at another hotel that same night. Alive and well. She began to look at the New York lights laying down facing the window. Leaning her head straight to the right looking, someone knocked on the door, she answered. It was Jerry she met downtown, she chuckles. Come on in. Jerry walks in differently, Chelsa looks at him a ruthless manner and smiles as he begins to look at her. Well, hi, Jerry nods. hi, handsome! Chelsa says with a smile. What do you do for a living, Chelsa? I'm a killer. She answered kissing him gently and moving him to the bed. How are you? He looked at her nervously. She began to kiss him. They kiss for hours. The door knocks again. Chelsa answers the door and gets hit by a girl that she didn't know. Chelsa hits back and slams her against the table and shoots her. Jerry looks at Chelsa and just cries over the girl that was his girlfriend. She grabs her backpack and leaves, she smirks at the door.

I WILL SEE YOU AGAIN. he yells back at her. She didn't do anything, she kept walking. No tears, no worries, no sorry. No nothing. She walks out the hotel building without a tear. People were walking in and out the New York hotel. She catches a taxi to the airport. The taxi goes through the dark ally where she suggested to him to go. Chelsa rolls her window down and gives Kerry and Jerry their cut. The man that was crying for his girlfriend. She paid him in full and Kerry in full. Chelsa drove off and just smiled. The taxi driver got killed. Chelsa shot him and just pushed him out the car and drove off and just began to drive with blood on the car window. She wipes it off real good. She drove off. Picking off the drop and just picking up others. Where to? Chelsa asks as she talks to the passengers. Airport. they answered. Good. Chelsa answered differently and excitedly. They arrived at the airport. Chelsa waited until the passengers got out. They paid, received their change. Chelsa smileed as she shook their hands. Chelsa drives off and leaves 2 blocks down from the airport and just leaves the taxi car in a spot where there was no parking. She grabs her backpack and walks away in the dark street alone with a gun in her hand. She walks without fear. She runs as she begins to get the fun out of it. She stops running out of breath. She arrives at the front of the airport. She puts on her sunglasses and just begins to walk in. No long line. Just her. She walked up to him and just began paying in cash without the man saying where to, or how much. No nothing. Just money of 100's and 50's up front. The man didn't say anything. Just took the money. Where to? Miami. Private plane. Here is my card. The card went through. Your plane will come at 10:42. Here is your ticket. Thank you so much. She smiles back. He looks at him and he looks at her. A young cute guy she thought to herself, that was interesting. She walked off and had a seat. The man stared at her as she was looking at her phone. Staring at her phone and just becoming quiet as she starts to look at her Instagram and Facebook. Scrolling through Facebook as if she was looking for something. People posting about the human clone shooting that was made a couple of hours ago. She began to be more quiet and more different and silenced. People stared at her. She didn't stare back. The feeling of being noticed by a profile picture or her last name. There was 500 million out for her capture. Dead or found for 500 million. People wanted to catch her because her name was famous. Chelsa Vegan dead or alive.

She just continued to look at her phone, and began to look and stare into her screen while the technology was hurting her eyes. Someone came up to her. They sat by her and just watched. She noticed that people were watching and becoming bolder and bolder, not minding their business. She finally held a gaze and just began to look around. Nothing there. She grabbed her backpack and put it on her back. She goes to the bathroom. Reflection in the mirror, reflection everywhere. She stands one way and 4 of her reflections spread like a shadow. Didn't know what it was called but it was different. She sighed as she looked at herself differently. She just continued to stand there. She walked out and began to sit back down for hours and hours. She didn't talk or look. She did her business the way she was supposed to do. Just one look at her computer. The plane arrived at 10:00pm. She got on her private plane and just to enjoy the private moment alone, but something was off. She looked at New York city as the plane took off, she smiled and closed her eyes remembering her past. She looked at her phone, her and her husband Kevin popped out on her phone. Her skin started to peel as soon as another human clone like herself started to become activated by another inactive battery.

A battery has to be changed within a month or two if not used properly but for human clones the batteries lasted up for a year or more. Humans don't need batteries but dolls and toys have to be charged or changed despite the toy or doll and for the humans. The human technology lasted up to 5 to 6 years but with updating software and technology the robots can misbehave improperly to any software.

3

TECHNOLOGY MADE TO CONTROL

The university of New York was having a session about humans and technology since everything that has transformed into a clone murdering. For the students that were science and technology majors needed to know about the technology that were out and for most of them they wanted to change degrees but was hoping their courses wouldn't change.

The professor John Cape Taten walked onto the stage with a grey silk tailormade suit. Everyone was silent, the room was dark but the screen of the computers.

As we know technology has been here for decades. When did this technology start? How long has it been here? Well, my friends, my fellow peers. No one knows that answer. We can search on Google, Yahoo, Bing and etc for the answer but do we really know how long it has been here? This is just the basics of when it was invented. Technology was made to have easy access to things in general. Now we have technology to control the mindset of humans by acting as humans but responding like clones. Nobody knows who is who and who is what. You could be sitting by a clone now. Students laugh but the professor didn't. Do we know who we are sitting by? The professor asked. The other scientists brought out another human that looked just like him. People murmured amongst themselves asking each other what was going on but nobody knew. It was a speechless act that had everybody on the edge of their seat. Now I have no brothers or sisters. I grew up by myself. Me, myself and I. Nobody else, of course I had parents, but no twin. You may be thinking is this my twin? The answer is No. No, I don't.

This is professor John, the other me but the technology of me. He follows what I do, what I see, and how I act. He is the reflection of me but he is built as a human. Now, if I murder him, it would be like murdering myself but myself is made out of clone. The only person that can access this clone is by my own DNA. Blood.

The professor cuts his arm gently. Everybody gasps. The clone opens up to a robot accessed with technology to turn off and on. Whoever made this clone, whoever builds clones by real humans are being held against their will.

The technology hospital was losing clones one by one as they marched down the street like soldiers. Different human clones. Different personalities walking on each side of the street.

One drop of blood that's all it took., to have your personality, your mindset, your dreams and goals are in one drop of blood and all. Nobody will ever know. Robots VS humans. Human clones vs Human. Who will win? If they bleed. They are human, if they don't. They are clones.

Miami at 4am. Chelsa arrives safely at her destination. The plane landed on solid ground. Hello, Miami! She said as she stepped off the plane. She begin to stare at the sky. She walks to her limo with her guards. She begin to tsk at them throwing her bags at them and begin to get in the car. She hugs her husband Vega. Vega gave Chelsa his wife 890K up front. Thanks baby! He says smoking his cigar almost lit his pants. Be careful! Chelsa says sipping her wine. I don't want you to lose yourself into the business. I want you to become a model! Is that an demand? Chelsa asked, rolling down the windows, taking a breath. I will do it. They arrived at the model show. You got 3 hrs before the show ends. He says as he began to walk in with her mink coat. She walks in the room with all models staring at her. Who are you? Asked one of the models. Who are you? Asked Chelsa.

Leave me alone. I said who are you? The model demands by pushing her down and kicking her. Chelsa didn't say anything but busted her throat and the model was dead. The models looked at the model that has been killed by Chelsa but Chelsa didn't give another look. She kills the models with her sword and it was just her on the stage with her red long Dolce and Gabbana dress, 8 inch heels, red lipstick, silk white skin glowing into the spotlight as people snapped pictures on phones, and cameras. Blood dripping from the stage. Nobody noticed. She walked like a pro model and did 3 hours of modeling. Officers walked up to her without warning, grabbed her harshly off the stage.

4

LET ME RE-INTRODUCE MYSELF

The officers brought Chelsa in, grabbing her by her arms, yanking her. Unconscious, drugged and unaware she didn't know what was happening. When she was awake, it was cloudy, she couldn't see straight. All she could see was a male officer standing by a woman agent that was sitting down. The officers jerked her up quickly. Chelsa vomited while she was being forced to sit up.

The woman across from her folds her arms and watches. Not giving any remorse or empathy. The woman opens up her file, smirking at the file she had on Chelsa Vegan.

Are you ready to answer some questions? Asked the woman agent. Chelsa sits up, lowering her head and then back up as soon as she sobered up from the drugs that was given to her.

Oh, I'm sorry, let me introduce myself, The agent said but before she even got the chance to speak. Chelsa interrupts. No, let me introduce myself. Chelsa said as she gets up hitting the officers with the chair, using their own guns for their own murder. The other officers were slow to take their guns out or either their guns got stuck in their holsters.

I didn't introduce myself properly, casually, I'm a killer. I'm 5'9, medium size, and an executive of Vega's Enterprise. I'm the best there is. Nobody can take my place, a wife, a mother and the best kick ass boxer, joined when I was 18, now I'm 24 and ready to conquer. Now, that's me, Chelsa MClinta Liuta Vegan. I took my husband's name for his money. I get paid 999k per month by staring at people and judging them. She laughs as she tells the cameras that were recording. Chelsa said as she shoots the agent. Chelsa sits down as she leans her head back glancing at the ceiling. Two shots and one man falls down with his camera. The sirens goes off.

Chelsa walks slowly with a shotgun on the side of her, face bloody. Officers runs on each side of the halls. Each and every one of them were dead. The clones started to match on the side of her. The helicopter made it on the top of the roof. Chelsa had a photoshoot to be at in another hour. The helicopter flies around the city.

5

GETTING CAUGHT

Chelsa walks in, the boss took one big glance and needed a break, 5 min break everyone. The boss says as she gets up giving her consultant the moment to absorb the boldness that she just saw. She smiles as she began to get her some cookies and donuts. Pounelle England walks in the building with a long white dress on, flats, and long purple hair. Hello, Cousin! Chelsa says by hugging her. Where is the family? See? I'm polite to children and to family. That's nice to me, Chelsa says as she talks to the reporters. Cameras were on Pounelle and Chelsa. Did you ask? Chelsa yells. DID YOU

ASK TO TAKE PHOTOS? OR DID YOU JUST TAKE THEM? Don't! Make me shoot your ass. Chelsa says as she shoots his ankle in front of everyone, including Pounelle and her family. Chelsa looks at Pounelle and smiles. Sorry! He asked for it! Chelsa begins. What are you doing today? Asked Chelsa. Nothing much. Just making money! How about you Champion? Nothing much. I'm taking you out. Chelsa says as she begin to get her wallet. Chelsa held Pounelle's hand as they walked out. Jon begin to tsk and began to see differently. Jon began to wave. Chelsa is kin to Pounelle? Asked Vegan. Jon didn't answer. He began to sip his wine that was giving to him. Jon cocked his neck gently to the right just as the others were doing. What are you doing here, Jon? This is not the place for you. Vegan says. How about this?

Jon how about what? Your money? No, I'm not here for that. I'm not here for anything. I'm here to support my wife. So, if you gentlemen and ladies would excuse me. I have a wife I have to meet.

Vegan: Guard the door

Jon tsks and breaks both arms of both men. and chopped the head off with the fence sword that was near. And threw it on the ground and walked out clean with no blood on his Men's Wearhouse suit that he loved so much. Jon glanced over his shoulder and there was a big suitcase of gold and money, he picked it up and walked with two passports in his hands. Vegan begin to grab the sword on the throne of his table, his father's sword that was in the generation of the Vegan family. Jon! Be a man and fight! Turn around and face me! Vegan said as he threw the sword to Jon. Jon sighed. You and your cornbread, chicken wing no good big bones. Jon says as he snorts a laugh, but walked swishing the sword back and forth with his right hand, left hand business suitcase. Let's do this then! Jon says as he knocks the sword out of Vegan's hands. Is there a point to this? Says Jon with a smile. Come on, we family! We shouldn't be doing this and besides I got you this time. Hahahaha! Jon and Vegan laughed. Help me up please? Jon helped Vegan. Want to drive the Ferrari? Jon says to Vegan. Car race? Asked Vegan

Vegan, 900 million up front?

Jon nods and walks to the car. I wonder what our women are talking about? Ha! Money! What you think, Jon? They begin to race in the streets where people can see. While the women were having lunch in a public restaurant. How is it in Miami? Pounelle asked gently, staring at a different reflection she saw in her cousin. It's good. Different people stare, and just want me to do it back. Do you really get paid 999K just for staring?

What do you stare at to get paid? Chelsa did not answer. She just began to look at Pounelle. Talk to me, Chelsa! I miss you racing with me Cousin!. One of the fans yells and just runs to Pounelle and Chelsa.

One of the fans yells and just begins to talk to them both. Chelsa MClinta? Wow, nice to see you! How is business? Business is good. Chelsa answered slightly and beautiful. Pounelle stares at her for a second and just begins to stare. Looking at different expressions that became different. Are you going to still ride in the Derby? You know what, I don't know yet, maybe I will make a comeback. What you think?

Pounelle shook her head. All three of them laughed and yes, I think I will make a comeback soon. The fan smiles. Want some water? Chelsa asks her fan. Pounelle looked at Chelsa and Chelsa looked at Pounelle. Horse Race? Asked Chelsa.

Pounelle raised an eyebrow gently. Soon as you think. They were there at the derby breaking in. They raced and got caught.

6

GETTING AWAY

Jon, Vegan, Pounelle and Chelsa gets caught by Police officers at the same time. All of them lined up against the car, staring at each other. They cock a smile on their faces. The Policemen looked at all of them with a smile. "Y'all something else". Lord have mercy!

"Lord give me strength".

Pounelle: Officer? officer? She says two times

Officer, "What?"

Can we go?

Yes, you can go. The officer said gently with a smile getting back to his car. They move quickly. Ladies would you like to explain. What were you doing at the Derby?

Pounelle said, "breaking in. Lord! Vegan said!

Chelsa shakes her head as she slowly grabs her gun but other officers arrived. Were they human? Shootings occurred. Chelsa continued to stand there writing them a check.

They begin to drive and just heading to the mall to shop and besides I won. So, pay up, Pounelle says with her left hand out. Chelsa gets her checkbook. $456,789,878.00. There you are! Both couples won the dish out.

7

JON'S VICTORY

New York January 31, 2030 at 12:35 PM. The Horse racing was ready to begin. Chelsa was being a different person altogether as she began to be next to Pounelle. The man that begins to say that numbers. The announcer rings the bell. He began to understand the riders. Pounelle and Contrnelle in the lead with 50 point. Asian in the Lead with 30 catching up at Pounelle. Jon and Vegan with suits watching their women go and make money. I bet Pounelle will win Asian and Buck, Jon stares at the bundle of cash. Deal. Jon says with a smile and shaking the old man's hand. Jon England and yours? Are you Pounelle's husband? My name is Jack Bolden! Nice to meet you, Jon! All three men stood with respect and wisdom as they sat in VIP section. Jon clears his throat and answers. Everyone yells and cheers as Pounelle wins the first 3 ways.

Jon! Da! He speaks in Russian Excited. Da! Very good! Everyone in VIP voted for Asian and Victora but Jon. All the men and women stared at Jon! They paid up. $900K+900K+$990+ $470K and more that was given to Jon. Jon smirks and leaves with dough of money in his left suit pocket.

8

FIGHTING FOR YOURSELF

Chelsa began to model that same night as the derby begins Models dead, blood not showing at all. Chesla smirks as she begins to walk into her hotel taking off her wig that she wore for the time of the night. She wiped her tears as she began to cry harder, and harder. She wipes her lipstick, and then washes her face. Vegan came in the house drunk. Are you drunk? Get your clothes on, you will do what I say! Vegan says pulling her arm. Chelsa snatches away gently and looks at him. He slaps her demanding her to put on the dress. She gets a grip and hits him with his shoe and then a pan with grits by the kitchen. She was quick to shoot him. The room service knocked on the door. No answer. The police officer was in that hallway section and heard another gun shot. She shot the models and then shot the room service.

9

MAMA'S NOTE AND TEACHINGS

The door was wide open, Chelsa sitting on the bed. Never let a man hit you. When they hit you, They may feel like they own you. Nobody owns you unless you let them. You give them power to what you want them to have. As Chelsa goes back in memory to what she would have said to her children as she hugs them. You build yourself who you want to do and be. Love you! You don't need a man to do that for you. Come here, babies! Look in the mirror, know who you are. Be you! Understand you, love you, care about you! Don't worry about the world as long as I'm here. You won't have to be touched. Look at me! You my world! Don't let nobody touch you. Nobody will take nothing from you. God got you! The children read on into the notes. Hold your head up! Mama is with reflection. That knife cut through his wrist and as she remembered his heart is where he breathed. Chelsa stopped herself before she ended up murdering her own lover.

The officers comes in and takes her slowly while she still had on the red dress and heels. Bodies on the floor. Reporters took photos as she walked slowly to the lobby and into the police car as they waited for her.

10

FIRST DEGREE MURDER

Judge Mason arrives at the bench and the court arises. Kora was getting ready for school for the first time. Reporters were waiting outside of their house. Kora takes a deep sigh before she even got in the car that was waiting for her.

The two drivers were waiting to kill Kora Vegan once they got into the highway forest. They were blaming everyone in the vegan family for the murders that were committed in that family. Even though Kora didn't really murder anyone at the time. She got blamed for her last name. Since she was adopted by her auntie Chelsa. Kora took after the name Vegan since she was the only family member she knew.

They didn't go by their plan to murder her but somebody was waiting to murder the people that were going to murder her but to make it look like she did it but that wasn't the case. Kora quickly ran out the car, running to the school yard before the school bell rung. Why did they want to frame Kora? Why did they want to kill her? Did someone knew who she was? The questions were valid but who saw the murderers? They were around the school somewhere hiding out. Everybody in that school stood by each student. One student sliced a cut to her arm once she walked into the school. Fresh blood was like prey to theses student and Kora could tell it was going to be one hell of a year and semester. Kora walked to the bathroom. Two to three bodies fell out of the bathroom stall and one body nailed to the wall.

Kora stood still, nodding her head as she accepted the fact that she was going to be the bitch they always wanted but never was. The children were waiting outside the bathroom door, cornering her.

11

LIVE

Notes was placed on Blena's table. She opens the note and it was by her love of her life. The note was folded in 3 ways. She opens and reads the later.

Dear, Blena

You are my world, you are my joy, you are my everything. I guess I will let you know who I am. I am an killer that works for his father. Please don't be disappointed in me but I kills for a living. My first assignment was last night. I'm a Business Contracter. I love passing technical contract papers.

I been on my own for 10 years, taking care of family and putting my mother, my sister through college. My little brother is learning how to play soccer and wants to go to the pro's. I'm making more money as a killer. Than what my father was giving me. Grandma needs her attention. I love you for you only. I brought my family a house over in Alaska and they love it. If you want to leave here and go to Alaska. I have a master in real estate and can become anything. I love you and become you. I did everything in my day. I traveled and became your husband. You my world and I'm proud to become that. We shall live everyday.

Ivan was right at the window waiting for her to come to him. He comes in and hugs her. Let's get out of here. Let's live together. Let's go travel, he says as he packed her things she was going to need. You know what, leave it. We can buy new things. She says with a smile. They both ran and into the hummer they left. They began to ride and ride all day and all night. They went on the north side, east, and west. They were on the coast. Ivan drove and drove.

12

LOVE

They stopped and rested. Ivan pulled up to the Safeway gas station. Filled the car up with 20 gallons or over. It was $18.20. He paid it and got snacks. Blena came in and got snacks as well. 8 packs of different gums, 20 bags of chips, 15 packs of meat, drinks and other things that they eat everyday. Ivan paid for everything and told her to keep her money and save it. I will buy it, baby. He says with a smile. And the add on was a total of $397.98. He paid $400 up front and got change back. He smiled and carried the bags out. Be back. 2 hours of shopping. Blena didn't say a word but just looked at him.

He smiles as he starts the car. He drives off to the highway. They drive for hours. Blena still awake and was just staring at him. We are almost there, honey. She smiles and continued to watch. He pulls to the hotel in Oregon. We are traveling baby. No matter what, I'm here. He says stopping the car, parking it. She gets out the car and so does he. She goes to the room and gets undressed and puts on a dress. The dinner on top of the building was already ready. He waits at the door as she comes out. My Lady, He says giving her his arm. They walk to the elevator and goes up to the top of the roof. They see Oregon from where they were standing. He pulls the chair for her and just smiles. He pulls the chair for him. Ivan began to serve her first and then him. They enjoy. The violinist plays romantic music as they become one with love and with each other. They began to share a noodle together. He gives her his last meatball and cake. He didn't hesitate at all. He gave it all to her. Want to dance? Ivan says with a smile. He holds her and rocks back and forth as the music plays. She dances on his toes and they bring harmony. The violinist started to cry. They begin to kiss and kiss. Into love they go. The butler came in with a package that was a box. Something moved. What moved? Ivan says with a smile. The puppy moved the box. The puppy cries and cries. She holds the puppy and the puppy feels the love that was given.

13

KORA'S DOLL MARKS

Chelsa begins to fly to the next country. Kora was playing with her dolls. Music of Melanie Martine'z Teddy Bear was playing on Repeat. Kora smirks and marks the doll with her pen. As the pen almost hits the doll. Chelsa was killing everyone in another country. Kora felt that and whoever was in the way was going to be shot. The blond hair doll was stabbed. The 5 year old girl Kora proceeding loudly but quietly. She stabs her big sister because she wanted to be the only little girl. Kora's big sister Coraine was mean and cruel when she was left alone. Coraine was a blond doll to Kora. The song plays on Repeat as she tiptoed to the room where Coraine was. The song was played loud. Coraine and Blena was smoking and doing weed as they were sitting on the bed. Blena knew something was going to happen. Blena goes to the bathroom. What are you doing in here asked Coraine as she threw a teddy bear at Kora. Kora comes in and stabs Coraine. 18 times and didn't stop when Blena came in. Blood on the wall and on Kora's face. Kora didn't have remorse for her sister at all. Kora smiles at Blena. Blena looks at her and then looked at the body. Shhhh! Kora says with a bloody face. She tastes the blood and places the doll on Coraines stomach and the knife in the left hand to make it look like a suicide.

14

BETRAYAL TO THE COP

The cops came in the house without knocking. Kora waited for the cop to come in. She smiles at him and looks at him. Ivan waited for him too. This is the cop that killed my sister's husband. Which is my best friend. Tells Ivan to Blena as they sit in the bloody smelling room as they watch the cop from there. Ivan smiles as the cop arriving at the doorstep. Blena distract the cop with your sex appeal and bring him in here. He is a sick Motherfucker. He won't care about someone's body. Blena pulls Kora back but Kora runs to food storage. Blena unbuttons her T-shirt and her pants. She puts her pants down by the couch. The police officer comes in the house.

The police officer takes off his sun glasses and smacks his gum. Looking at Blena. Ivan watches from afar. She walks up to him and kisses his lips. He looks at her amazed. She guide him to the bloody smelly room and Ivan was right. The officer didn't notice or didn't want to notice. Lookie, lookie, here. Blena says with a smile. So, what? A bloody body. And? Let's get back to you, he says. Hold this knife. Anything you want. He says with a smile. Be back baby. Kiss kiss goodnight. Blena says walking with Ivan and Kora. Ivan had the triplets in the car. Nice going baby! Ivan says with a smile. They were ghost before the cops came. The cop that was in the room with the bloody body. He wasn't aware to put the knife down or to wipe it. So they caught him and put him in prison for life.

15

EMPTY HOUSE

Chelsa pulls up to the house she always knew, the head lights of the car remained on. Getting out the car slowly with her heels, walking to the steps, stepping on each step, heels clinching to the wooden porch. Door creaking. The door fell apart as soon as it was touched. The house was empty. Where was the family? Kora was taken away with the child protective services. Chelsa was alone in the house again. Blena and Ivan went their ways, Coraine was dead and everybody she loved was slipping away from her except for her father that she hardly liked but loved deeply. The phone rings twice as she stands in the middle of the living room. It was just an abandoned wooden house.

16

I KILLS CAUSE I WANT TO

A call comes through at 3:36 Am. A call from her stepdad that treated her and her mother badly. A step father that only loved ass instead of her. Did he ever felt remorse? About him stabbing my brother and leaving him for dead. I don't know where my other brothers are but when I find them, I'm killing them too. I loved Noah with all my heart. My brother Noah would play at the river. He would treat me as human. Love me like a human. So, did mama. That's why I'm there from a distance. Nobody in my family had remorse. No love, no kindness or anything. Just a plain old selfish man that cared about himself. Chelsa wrote in her dairy. Placing it on the table before she went to see her stepdad early at 3:46am. She arrived at his doorstep. He answers. Come on in! He hits her with the door because he wanted to. He saw her but didn't say sorry. So what she did was nothing. She shoots him as his back was turned and shoots him twice to make sure he was dead. I kill cause I want to. She gave the word right back to him and left the house with the stove on. The house blows up and no remorse from Chelsa. She drives by shooting people's homes and them. She laughs hysterically as the car rolls over and hits the ground.

BRUTAL BETRAYAL

SEQUEL TO TO BE YOU

INTRODUCTION

It was Kora first time at school. Pelia placed all her school supplies on the table, her pencil box, crayons, colored pencils, papers, and bender and all on the table. Kora had to organize things herself, and Implicitly, she didn't hesitate, the other kids were inside the van before anything. Amelia was handicapped, couldn't move fast like the others did, but Kora was right behind her, walking with her, making sure she was alright, instead of rampant. Nobody checked on Amelia. Kora was just waiting to kill. While the car pulled up to this fancy school, Kora looked around, saw some kids that were rancid, some were abhorrent as she went inside the school, the world that she knew, that was her type, cruel and difficult was her type. Before she stepped into an unknown world, she took a deep breath, glanced around, sniffed the air, got used to the feeling since she was going to stay there for two years. A high society school was famous around the state, plus they do horse training at the school, the other room, learning how to cook, for those who don't know how to cook was studying in the other room, Amelia made a joke as she passed by Kora going to her class slowly, heading up the stairs, and to the right. Kora followed suit but slowly up the stairs. Going straight to the ladies room, the ladies room was different, a waterfall by the mirror was pretty but something else wasn't pretty. A blond hair stabbing another female student in the stomach. Kora wasn't watchful for who was behind her. Hi! An unknown voice came back behind Kora. Kora didn't like anyone sneaking up on her for the fun of it, if she wasn't doing anything wrong, nobody shouldn't be that damn bold. This girl that was the same age as Kora was right up in Kora's personal space. Can you give me some space, please? But the girl didn't. She stood there with the school books in her hand. A white girl that was popular that owned everything, a white girl that was popular than everyone in the school thought it was okay to sneak up on a known international killer that could kill any second. If you come wrong, she will kill you just for being cocky for no reason. Kora gave her the same attitude but then the girl finally let her ego go and decided to walk away and not say nothing. Kora took a deep sigh and then went inside her locker and placed her bag in it, her books and stuff too. The same girl that was sneaky was right beside the locker. I decided to come, be human and talk to you, Kora. If you don't mind! She said in a rough way but Kora looked at her calmly, trying not to show her ass to a known ass school. It's okay. You can talk to me. I'm sorry where are my manners? My name isKeulla what is yours?

My name is Kora

Clia: Kora what?

Kora froze for a second, looking down at her notes. Wondering if this was a test or anything that would get her thrown back to the system.

My name is Kora Vegan

Vegan? Keulla says shocked, face begrimed, face turning red with purple looking like she had eczema. The feeling of obsession was there between those two but Kora didn't realize it. She just allowed what it was to be just that, what it was. Anyway, you know my father Johnny Demita? No, I haven't heard that name before. well he goes to this school, and also he owns half of this state. Is that right? Kora says not impressed or anything. Keulla folds her arms and gives a look like "I'm better than you kind of look". Kora closes her locker and then goes to her seat in the classroom. She was the only one in the classroom. The teacher that was supposed to be coming was dead with the female student that was killed by the students that went to the school. Two people were dead in one day, another student will be dead if no one catches the killer in time.

CHAPTER 2

Before they could have found the killer, the private school was on lock down for now. They started to question the students each one by one but the police didn't have any witnesses about the killing of an innocents of one adult and a child. It was a guess. Students wanted to know who did what to whom but some of the children didn't answer, I guess because they didn't know the answer but those who did, stood back and watched as the school was about to have a riot. As the school was about to have a riot, Kora started to walk around but wasn't watchful. The only problem Kora had was being treated differently because she was a ruthless killer, that would kill anyone who got in her way, or wouldn't have the decency to let go of something that didn't need to be dealt with. She wouldn't kill because someone disagreed with her, she would just disappear. When she kills, she disappears.

Keulla watched Kora as she was walking around the school yard field twice, looking at the phone, texting someone but Clia didn't know. Keulla wanted to know what Kora was up to, so she just followed Kora, instead of coming up to her asking what was she doing knowing that there were other students on their phones doing stuff they had no business doing but when someone is suspicious about something or someone, they going to act on it, knowing that person isn't bothering them. Keulla walked up to Kora but Kora didn't move or anything, she just looked at Kora. Keulla folded her arms, and then just stared but Kora kept walking and Keulla kept following. Kora seemed like she didn't mind but when she did. Kora walked over to the police officer and stood by them. Keulla turned to the opposite direction. Kora made a grin. On Kora phone was some money being transported across the boarder, the police was standing right next to Kora. Someone could have glanced at Kora's phone and got some information from there but nobody was around to see. Keulla's father was running low on funds, the schools he owned was running out of money, books and other supplies the students needed. Kora found that out by paying someone to hack inside her father's secrets and claim it into her name. The board of the school was looking for someone to take charge and that's what she was going to do. Challenge is not easy, not hard. you just need to lay low some of the time, and I think one of these times, I must lay low, Kora said talking on the phone with one of her hacker men that would do anything for Kora.

Kora nodded as her plan worked perfectly and brilliantly. Now my money. Keulla heard. Who is that? Kora didn't answer with the banker, she tranferred half of a billion to his savings account, she still had enough money in there to fulfil her dreams, go to college and live a long life. In other words, she was set for life. Didn't need any help or anything. she wanted everything, just like Keulla did but Keulla would kill her own teammates just because she could. The Vegan family just didn't kill for no reason, they had a reason sometimes. Keulla wanted to secretly kill Kora Vegan, the thrill killer, but she didn't know how, neither did Kora. Kora finally met her match but didn't want to admit it. Why should she praise a girl her own age? Who was Keulla, God?. Kora didn't praise anyone that were people, she only praised God for keeping her alive. It is God that gives and takes away.

Kora walked around Keulla as Keulla was still standing there, waiting for a response but didn't get it. Kora had to be someone at 4:30 sharp and couldn't waste no time. She walks to her locker, gets her bags, she already wrote down her homework assignment, and everything. Had her i phone in her hand walking heavy steps as she passing saying excuse me to the students that was passing pass and not saying excuse me back. Rudeness was not one of Kora's favorite either. she couldn't understand it. Kora skips to her car and then drives off. Keulla tried to keep up but since Keulla didn't have the courage to say what she was going to say, Kora spoke for her by doing something Keulla knew she wouldn't like.

CHAPTER 3

Keulla arrived to her home but it seemed like there was no one home to go to, cause Keulla's father was packing their stuff. Keulla mother had cancer and she was dying from it. Keulla had a surprise waiting for her in the house. Keulla father was in tears. We have to move somewhere else, somewhere our money could afford. I'm sorry but we have to move somewhere else. Why? but all my friends are here, where would that put me? her father didn't answer. She rushes into the house, into the living room she goes in to, finds Kora sitting on the couch, drinking tea out of Keulla's favorite cup. Kora nods gently as she gives a smile. Keulla's dad comes in, this is Kora, she heard about the school board's situation and that we were losing our students, and that she would help us look for a home.

Where is our home located again? asked Keulla's father. Kora takes another sip and then speaks passionate about her plan for them but it was the intention that she had. Kora talked about her plans, as time passed by. Kora calls the hospital and then pays someone to kills Keulla's mother. They do it. She frustrates her dial pad but the device that she was using turned off, so with the other phone she had, she made a phone call to the police, saying that someone was going to kill the Ambassador of the schools that was owned by Keulla's father. which was the mother of Keulla Malia. She turned off the phone that she used to call the police, took the battery out and then threw it in the garbage but kept the battery. It was a setup to those who kept their word to Kora. Kora was a snake that would bite for the blood of it. Kora smiled as she parked across the street waiting to see what would happen. Kin was the doctor that was going to kill Malia, since that was his assignment by Kora. He did just that, then called the house that Keulla was in and then say that she died. Making up a lie but it was brutally planned like Keulla planned to kill Kora but Kora made her first move and now she was just waiting for Keulla to make hers.

CHAPTER 4

It was a set up from the start. The doctor that pulled the plug was under arrest, after Kora had promised that nobody would get caught. The police would have never known unless someone knew or someone had a secret camera in the room where the patient was unconscious and was in a nervous condition. The plug was pulled. Didn't let the family members know or anything. Kora smirks was unagreeable but kept a smile cause betrayed one of her own people, took back the money that she gave the worker that helped pull the trigger. She didn't even put it in the bank account after the job was done. She was a snake alright. When the doctor got to the police station, fingerprints were taken and all. Took him to his cell but he was killed before the next morning. Kora had the money to pay inside the prison and out. The sources she had meant that she wasn't going to play nice, mess with her, the people you love will have to pay for the mistakes you made that didn't have to be, just if you would just think before hurting Kora. You will be just fine. Keulla was ready for revenge but Kora owned Keulla and her family without her even knowing it.

CHAPTER 5

Since the world is fucked up and cruel. Let's talk about being cruel. Keeping someone from getting an education because they don't believe that J.F. Kenndy was a racist piece of shit. The students on campus was having a deep unusual conversation cause the subject in school was about racism and different things that the world looks at, or count on or whatever society decided to do regarding their gender or sex. Nobody was happy or safe at the school that they were in. Society had their own private meetings and stuff. Launch was whatever you brought from home. Some students that were there for a long, long, long time didn't have to pay at all. So, some went down the street and got a hamburger. Just cause they went to a popular school, didn't mean they had to eat like one. That's how people got bullied for being different. The people that were their didn't like to eat salad or proper food just because they had money. Some liked to eat hearty, meaning having french fries, and all that stuff. If people thought like this, nobody would have any enemies for being different. Different doesn't mean not human. Just means that their minds are different, they know what they want and how they want it. The school was almost half empty cause the other students was across the way eating. The group society was having a meeting to target the ones that were not in their organization. Who came up, was Kora Vegan. She was a threat to the group, or should we say to Keulla. Before the meeting started. Keulla started to gossip, and tell the whole school that Kora was a stalker but didn't say what she was. Keulla was a straight up criminal like she was but in her eyes, the wrong that she did, didn't matter as long as she didn't get caught. Like it is called society. Society will pick who is guilty and who is not, because of their skin tone, the way they look, where they lived was part of what society looked at, instead of looking at them as human and say that "this person is human, why hurt them if they haven't done anything wrong? why bully them cause they were different? nothing could or can be answered but a blank stare or a whatever attitude. Kora was one of the intimidating people on the list, one of the VERY RARE people on the list.

Keulla slaps the desk with the ruler, trying to get everyone's attention. Of course Kora was in the room listening, when she saw the photo of her, she smiled peacefully. She was excited about people getting excited about getting rid of her. She wasn't like the other Vegan's. Popular talked about. Kora sat in the back, I mean way in the back where nobody could see. Ladies and Gentlemen Thank you for coming to the meeting that we have every Wednesday. Thank you for coming! What we are here for is to target those who are new to this school, target those who are new because the new students now are not the same like they used to, It is rare that new students are coming. The other schools that my father owns is very popular then the other schools here in this town. One of the students that was in that room cleared their throat in attention. Yes, Jason what is it? Oh, It was nothing. something was caught in my throat.

Jason, just spit it out. What do you want to say? Why is Kora.
Kora

Keulla: Kora Vegan! Yes, what about her?

Jason: She is Beautiful! Nice tits and everything! Kora smiles in the back as she focuses hard again getting back to concentration. Jason's future girlfriend tapped him hard where he would feel it. She pulled down her tank top and shown half of her breast to him. He looked but was more fascinated with Kora's. Keyua rolled her eyes and then looked the other way, tried to zoom in but it made it more obvious. Keulla accidentally zoomed in towards her breast, Instead of her face. All the boys in that meeting sighed uncomfortably, trying not to get heated over a pair of breasts that they couldn't have. So, they took a deep breath and then shook their heads. Kora smiles again but then focus again. Seemed like Keulla's plan didn't work well this time but Keulla kept going with the meeting but the meeting was really about Kora and how she was a threat to the schools that her father owned. which was not true. Everyone knew that she was a phony that was spoiled and wanted power but went about it the wrong way. She was pompous and didn't want anyone to tell her anything. She didn't know what she wanted, so that's why she killed a girl to get her dream job, and then killed a guy cause he wasn't like her and that was all before Kora got there. I guess the bottom line was Kora wasn't like her, Kora didn't kill for the fun until later on, when Ivan didn't pay her and when her parents didn't want her, and her sister didn't accept her and abused her. This situation is and was part of some people's families, maybe not too extreme or anything but some families have a hard time accepting. Kora was a natural born killer. She decided to become a killer so that's what she did but now, that she is older and more wiser. She wants an education and she should get it no matter how hard her pass was or what she used to do. She was willing to put in the hard work and everything. Although she had money to have the school shut down if she wanted for being racists and controlling school, but Kora wanted to make their lives a living hell like they are making hers right about now.

CHAPTER 6

Kora stood still as a taser was right besides someone that was in the meeting. Kora didn't know anything until she looked through her scope to see the clouds, as the students were outside doing earth science, finding anything that belonged with earth. It was part of chemistry class and so forth and so on. Kora kept looking at her thick paper that she had on her board that she was holding to take notes. The teacher wasn't paying enough attention to the laser, so Kora spoke up, which she shouldn't have. She should have kept her mouth shut about the taser. The taser was against policy rules at the school. Tasers were a sign of violent behavior which included Gun violence. Mr. Sikes! There is a taser! Where? The teaser was right there on the side. Some other students saw it also but didn't say anything. Thank you for that Kora! Thank you for looking out but I don't see any laser. When he finally recognized, it was too late. One of the students was shot cold blooded on school grounds. Everyone was running for their lives, including kora but she ran the opposite. Come on, children! Mr. Sikes says as he was grabbing the children. The gun didn't seem to be turned off. Whoever was shooting the gun, knew what they were doing. Seemed like it was coming from the tree but who saw? Nobody. They finally got inside safe and sound. Police, the news and everyone that represented law enforcement and gossip news was there. It was a difficult time to bring the new children there. One of the students that was a target was head on shot. The new kids that were there and coming in were going to be dead before their two years were up at the high school. Somewhere 14 all the way up to 18. Their plan was to get rid of kids that didn't belong there. On Keulla's sake, she thought that nobody that was new belonged there. Mr. Sikes looked at Kora. Kora looked back. He looked frightened but calm. He didn't show any emotion. Since she was a Vegan, he was going to tell the people that were ahead of the school that she knew about it but didn't say anything. She had that student killed, which was nine that wasn't even on the list. Bullet flew without even caring if it hurted the other. The principle called Kora to the office and for what? Saving the ingrate students? Only 3 people got killed, someone was obviously planning that plot. Not Kora. They had that shit backwards. They should have sent out a search team for that type of stuff.